W9-APL-080

The Neat Pig

Once upon a time, there was a little pig
who liked to be neat.

He liked to sleep in a very clean bed.

He liked to eat from a plate.

And he liked to put on his neat, white coat.

"What are we going to do with Little Pig? He is too neat," said Mama Pig.

"We will teach him that pigs are messy," said Papa Pig.

So they made a mess of his bed.

They made him
eat in the grass.

And they put his neat, white coat in
the mud.

Little Pig was
very sad.

But then, Little Pig jumped up and
screamed, "I have a plan!"

So, Little Pig made all the beds very clean. He made a fine meal on nice plates. And he gave Mama and Papa Pig neat, white coats.

"Are you thinking what I am thinking?"
asked Mama Pig.

"Yes," said Papa Pig. "I *love* being neat!"

And the three pigs lived neatly ever
after . . .

Read it

. . . until Baby Pig came along!

Once upon a _____,

there was a little

_____ who liked to

be _____.

 He liked to

_____

in a very clean bed.

He liked to

_____

from a _____ .

And he liked to put on

his neat, white

_____

_____ .

"What are we going to do

with Little Pig? He is too
_____

neat," said _____

Pig. "We will teach him
_____

that pigs are _____,"
_____

said _____ Pig.

So they made a mess

of his

_____

_ _ _ _ _ _ _ _ _ _ _ _

_____ .

They made him eat in

_____

the _____ .

And they put his neat,

white coat in the

_____

_ _ _ _ _ _ _ _ _ _ _ _

_____ .

Little Pig
_____
- - - - - - - - -
was very _____ .

But then the little pig
_____
- - - - - - - - -
_____ up

and screamed,

"I have a
_____
- - - - - - - - -
_____ !"

So, Little Pig made all

the beds very _____.

He made a fine

_____

_____ on

_____ plates. And he

gave Mama and Papa Pig

neat, white _____.

"Are _____ thinking

what I _____ thinking?"

asked _____ Pig.

"_____," said _____

Pig. "I _____ being

neat!"

And the three _____

lived _____ ever

_____ . . .

. . . until _____

Pig came along!

Once upon a time, there was a little pig
who liked to be neat.

He liked to sleep in a very clean bed.

He liked to eat from a plate.

And he liked to put on his neat, white coat.

"What are we going to do with Little Pig? He is too neat," said Mama Pig.

"We will teach him that pigs are messy," said Papa Pig.

So they made a mess of his bed.

They made him eat in the grass.

And they put his neat, white coat in the mud.

Little Pig was
very sad.

But then, Little Pig jumped up and
screamed, "I have a plan!"

So, Little Pig made all the beds very
clean. He made a fine meal on nice
plates. And he gave Mama and Papa
Pig neat, white coats.

"Are you thinking what I am thinking?"
asked Mama Pig.

Draw it

"Yes," said Papa Pig. "I *love* being neat!"

And the three pigs lived neatly ever
after . . .

Draw it

. . . until Baby Pig came along!

Activities

Read it

Go on a reading scavenger hunt! Design a simple reading scavenger hunt for your child or student using written clues and books from around your house or classroom. Write the clues on a piece of paper, give the paper to your child or student, and then have him or her read the clues and find a book that matches each clue! You can write as many clues as you like, and you can even set a timer for your child or student as he or she gets really good at this activity! Here are some sample clues: Find a book with a long word in the title; find a book with at least five chapters; find a book about a president; find a book about a sports star; find a book with rhyming text; and so on.

Write it

Write a riddle! Ask your child or student to think of an item (for example, an animal, a food, a household object, a person, etc.) and to write three to five clues about that item. Have him or her read each clue, one by one, to friends or family to see if anyone can guess what the item is before running out of clues!

Draw it

Create a nature sketchbook! Have your child or student staple five or more blank pieces of paper together like a book. He or she can even make up a title for it. Ask him or her to sit outside or next to a window and draw things in nature such as a bird, a squirrel, an interesting rock, or a beautiful sunset. Your child or student should label his or her drawings and write the date for each nature entry!

A NOTE TO THE PARENTS:
When children create their own spellings for words they don't know, they are using **inventive spelling**. For the beginner, the act of writing is more important than the correctness of form. Sounding out words and predicting how they will be spelled reinforces an understanding of the connection between letters and sounds. Eventually, through experimenting with spelling patterns and repeated exposure to standard spelling, children will learn and use the correct form in their own writing. Until then, inventive spelling encourages early experimentation and self-expression in writing and nurtures a child's confidence as a writer.